W9-BYN-529

PABLO'S TREE

by **Pat Mora** • illustrated by **Cecily Lang**

SCHOLASTIC INC.

New York   Toronto   London   Auckland   Sydney

No part of this publication may be reproduced in whole or in part, or stored in a
retrieval system, or transmitted in any form or by any means, electronic,
mechanical, photocopying, recording, or otherwise, without written permission
of the publisher. For information regarding permission, write to
Macmillan Publishing Company, 866 Third Avenue, New York, NY 10022.

Text copyright © 1994 by Pat Mora.
Illustrations copyright © 1994 by Cecily Lang.
All rights reserved. Published by Scholastic Inc., 555 Broadway,
New York, NY 10012, by arrangement with Macmillan Publishing Company.
Printed in the U.S.A.
ISBN 0-590-67500-1

20 21 22 23 24 25   16 **5**   **21 22 23 24 25 26**

The text of this book is set in 14 point Leawood Medium.
The illustrations are rendered in cut paper with dyes.

In memory of my father, Raúl Antonio Mora,
and for a special boy

— P. M.

For Nicholas and his sunny smile

— C. L.

I'm ready, Mamá!" I say. "I'm ready for my birthday visit to Lito's. Hurry, Mamá! I want to see my tree."

I wonder if Lito, my grandfather, remembered. I wonder if he remembered to decorate my tree.

I ask, "Mamá, did Abuelito decorate my tree?"

"Your grandfather does not forget to decorate your tree, Pablo. Do you have your suitcase? What new birthday toys are you taking to Abuelito's?" asks Mamá.

"I've got my purple car, my book about whales, my tambourine, and my flute," I say.

Every year I spend the night after my birthday at my grandfather's house. We sit under my tree. We play with my new toys. Every year Lito decorates my tree for my birthday visit. Maybe my grandfather forgot.

"Are you sure he didn't forget?" I ask.

"I'm sure," says Mamá.

"Please tell me, Mamá," I say. "Tell me what Lito put on my tree. Is it lights? Is it little *piñatas*?"

Mamá smiles. "Pablo," she says, "don't you like surprises? Come. Let's go see your tree."

As we drive along I ask, "Is it little animals? Is it candy?" My mother just smiles and winks.

"Lito! Lito!" I say. "I'm here! I'm here!"

Lito opens the screen door. His face is happy, like a full moon. Lito gives my mother a kiss and a hug.

"Lito," I say, "I brought my new birthday toys. We can sit under my tree and play with my toys all day and all night."

Lito and my mother laugh.
"Pablo," says Lito, hugging me. "*¿Cómo está mi nieto grande?* How is my big grandson?"

I give Lito a giant hug. He almost falls down.
"Pablo!" says Mamá. *"Cuidado.* Be careful." But Lito
likes my giant hugs.

"Let's go see my tree," I say. "Hurry. Hurry, Lito." I
take Lito's hand and pull him to the back door.

When I see my tree, I run to it. I touch the tiny colored bells and wind chimes. "Ooooh," I say. I run around the tree, touching the bells and chimes. The wind blows and my tree jingles and rings.

I give Lito another giant hug, and again I almost knock him down. But he just smiles.

Mamá gives us each a good-bye kiss. We take her to her car. We put my suitcase in my room. Lito throws me an apple. We take the bag of toys out to the table under my tree.

Lito plays my flute. He says, "Pablo, do you remember the story of your tree?"

I run around and around my tree. I touch the branches so the bells and chimes ring. I shake my new tambourine.

"One day my mother came to this house," I say.

"Yes," says Lito. "Your mother said, 'I'm going to adopt a baby.' I went to the nursery down the street and bought a small tree. I said, '*Este árbol es para mi nieto*. This tree is for my grandson.'

"Your mother said, '*Ay*, Papá, what if the baby is a girl?' I said, 'I love little girls, but this tree is for my boy.'

" 'If it is a boy, he will have your name. He will be Pablo, too,' said your mother."

Lito stops and smiles. Then he asks, "What did we buy for the new baby, Pablo?"

"You and Mamá bought bottles and blankets for me," I say.

"Yes," says Lito, laughing. "We waited and waited for the phone to ring. We waited for the words 'Come for your baby.' I watered your tree, but I didn't plant it. I waited for you.

"First I put the little tree in the front yard near the sidewalk. 'No,' I said. 'This spot is too noisy for my boy's tree.'"

"And then you put it there, in the rose garden," I
say, "but you saw too many thorns. Then you put my
tree here."

"One day," says Lito, "the phone rang. Your mother
called. Her voice was full of smiles. She said, 'Papá,
guess what?' I said, 'When do I see my boy?' Your
mother laughed and laughed. She said, 'Papá, how
did you know?'

"I put your tree by the front door to welcome you. I washed my face and combed my hair.

"I looked out the window and waited for your
mother's car. I went out front and walked back and

forth on the sidewalk. Then I saw it. I watched your
mother lift you out so carefully.

"I looked at you and you looked at me. Your mother said, 'Hold him, Papá. Hold Pablo.'

"You fit just right in my arms. I said, 'Pablo, come and see your tree.' Then I said, 'Come. Let's plant Pablo's tree.'

"Your mother held you while I got my shovel and watering can," says Lito. "Carefully I dug a hole and planted your tree here. In the sun."

I say, "And the tree grew and grew. Like me."

"On your first birthday," says Lito, "I hung streamers on your little tree—yellow, orange, red. I carried you out to see them."

"And I grabbed them in my fist," I say.

"On your second birthday, I tied balloons of every color," says Lito. "You ran around and around your tree. I lifted you up to touch your balloons. You did not let me rest."

"On my third birthday, you put paper lanterns on my tree."

"And what was on your tree last year?" asks Lito.
"Birdcages," I say. "You put tiny birdcages all over
my tree. And this birthday is bells and chimes!"

I race around and around my tree. I touch the
branches and they ring.

Lito and I sit and listen to the wind. We listen to my
tree. We munch our apples.

I ask, "What will you put on my tree next year,
Lito?"

Lito chuckles and winks. "Pablo, that's a surprise."